A CHRISTMAS CAROL

Re-told by Anne McKie.
Illustrated by Ken McKie.

Once upon a time - on Christmas Eve - Ebenezer Scrooge sat busy in his counting-house.

A faded sign hung above his office door that read: "Scrooge and Marley". Jacob Marley had been Scrooge's business partner, but he had died over seven years ago, and Scrooge was such an old skinflint he wouldn't pay for a new sign to be put up.

It was cold, bleak, biting weather that day and the thick fog outside came pouring in through every chink and keyhole. But Scrooge never felt the winter chill, for he was a mean, tight-fisted old miser with a heart as cold as ice. He never did a kind deed or helped anyone, although he had piles of money locked away . . . and most of all he hated CHRISTMAS!

All day long Scrooge left his office door wide open to keep his eye on his clerk, Bob Cratchit, even on Christmas Eve. The poor fellow was so cold he had to work in his coat and scarf. And the fire Scrooge allowed him to have was so small it looked like one coal.

"A Merry Christmas, Uncle!" cried a cheerful voice. It was Scrooge's nephew, Fred, who had called to wish him the very best for the festive season.

"Bah!" cried Scrooge. "Humbug!"

"Don't be angry, Uncle. Come and share Christmas dinner with us tomorrow," said his nephew kindly.

The very word CHRISTMAS made Scrooge angry. "If I had my way," shouted Scrooge, "every idiot who goes around wishing people 'Merry Christmas', should be boiled with his own Christmas pudding and buried with a stake of holly through his heart. Keep Christmas in your own way and let me keep it in mine!" And Scrooge pointed to the door.

As he left, Fred stopped to wish Bob Cratchit a 'Merry Christmas'. The poor man was trying to warm his freezing hands by a candle flame.

The afternoon got foggier and darker and colder. A little boy bent down to sing a carol at Scrooge's keyhole, but at the first few notes of:

"God rest you, merry gentlemen,
May nothing you dismay!"

Scrooge grabbed his ruler and the poor boy fled in terror.

At last the time came to stop work and close the office. Bob Cratchit blew out his candle and put on his hat.

"I suppose you want all day off tomorrow," snapped Scrooge.

"If that's alright, sir," said Bob Cratchit timidly. "It's only once a year, and it is Christmas Day!"

"It is not alright!" replied Scrooge. "Just remember that I will have to pay you a whole day's wage for no work!" and Scrooge left with a growl.

Bob Cratchit locked up the office in a twinkling. On the way home - just because it was Christmas - he went down an icy slide twenty times, just for the fun of it!

Scrooge, on the other hand, ate his supper all alone at a nearby inn, and went home to bed.

He lived by himself in a dark old house that had once belonged to his partner, Jacob Marley.

Now, that Christmas Eve, as Scrooge put his key in the lock, he looked up, and instead of the brass door-knocker, he saw Marley's face!

As Scrooge stared in amazement, it turned into a door-knocker again.

At once Scrooge unlocked his door, and hurried inside and quickly lit a candle. Then he took a good look around all the rooms, just to make sure no-one was there. He even looked under the bed!

Quite satisfied, he locked his bedroom door and put on his dressing gown, his slippers and nightcap.

All of a sudden, an old bell that hung by the fireplace began to swing to and fro. Soon it began to ring out loudly - and so did every bell in the house.

Then Scrooge heard a different sound, as if someone was dragging heavy chains from the cellar, up the stairs and into his bedroom.

Poor Scrooge's knees began to knock and his teeth began to chatter as JACOB MARLEY'S GHOST floated through the door!

At first Scrooge thought his eyes were playing tricks, or his supper had given him indigestion. But the ghost did look like his old friend Jacob Marley, although it was covered from head to foot in chains, and loaded down with heavy cash-boxes, bunches of keys and big metal padlocks.

"I have come to warn you, Ebenezer Scrooge," wailed the ghost, "before it's too late!" And he rattled his chains at Scrooge.

"If you do not mend your ways at once, and become kind, loving and give to other people, you will end up like me!" the ghost went on. "In my life I cared for nothing but money. And look at me now. A lonely old ghost, deemed to wander around with nothing but money-boxes for company!"

Scrooge shuddered. "Tell me, dear friend, how can I change?"

By now the ghost was floating towards the window, his voice fading. "You will be visited by three Spirits when the clock strikes one. Listen to them, Ebenezer Scrooge, and you will escape my fate!"

And with that, the ghost of Jacob Marley floated out into the dark night and vanished among the chimney pots.

Feeling very tired, Scrooge closed the window, crept into bed and fell fast asleep.

A nearby clock struck midnight and Scrooge woke up. Feeling very nervous he lay awake until one. Would he see the first of the three Spirits - or had it all been a bad dream?

On the stroke of one, light filled the room. The curtains of his bed were drawn back and Scrooge found himself face to face with a ghost! It was a very strange ghost, small like a child, with long white hair.

"Who or what are you?" asked Scrooge.

"I am the Ghost of Christmas Past," said the Spirit in a gentle voice. "I am here to remind you of your past!"

The Spirit whisked Scrooge, still in his dressing gown and slippers, up in the air and out into the dark night . . . and back in time!

The city had vanished and they found themselves in a little country town. Scrooge was a boy again surrounded by his school friends.

All the boys were going home for the Christmas holidays. Sad to say, no-one came to fetch young Ebenezer that year. So he was left alone at school to spend a miserable Christmas all by himself.

When Scrooge remembered this he began to cry. The Spirit smiled and waved his hand. "Let us see another Christmas!"

Scrooge saw himself sitting in the schoolroom a few years later. Again all his friends had gone home for the Christmas holiday.

Suddenly, the door opened and his beloved sister, Fran, darted in. She flung her arms round his neck and kissed him.

"I have come to bring you home! Not just for the holidays, but for ever and ever!"

Quick as a flash, the Spirit whisked Scrooge away from his old school. In no time at all they were outside a warehouse door and the Spirit asked Scrooge if he knew the place.

"Know it! I was an apprentice there!" cried Scrooge excitedly.

They went in. Scrooge could see himself as a young gentleman, having a marvellous time at the office Christmas party.

His old boss, Mr. Fezziwig, had ordered all his young apprentices to stop work and join the family in fun and games. There was music and dancing and presents for all.

Poor Scrooge remembered how happy he had been in those days, but now he cared more about money than friends. And he had forgotten how to have fun.

The Spirit of Christmas Past had made Scrooge see what a lonely miserable old man he had become.

Suddenly Scrooge realised that he was back in his own bedroom. Tired out, he fell fast asleep.

All too soon he was awakened in the middle of a huge snore by a clock striking one.

As he peered over the bedclothes, Scrooge saw the whole place filled with rosy light from the next room.

Trembling, he got up and shuffled in his slippers to the door.

"Come in! Come in!" boomed a voice. "I am the Spirit of Christmas Present! Come in and get to know me!"

Scrooge entered timidly, and what a sight met his eyes. The room was full to bursting with Christmas fayre. And right in the middle sat a cheery fat giant of a ghost.

"Touch my robe!" said the Spirit of Christmas Present.

Scrooge did as he was told and held on tight.

Everything in the room vanished and Scrooge found himself walking through the cold snowy city streets together with the Spirit.

It was Christmas morning and the shops were still open. The grocer's, the baker's, the poulterer's and the fruit shops. All selling Christmas food right up to the very last minute.

Church bells rang out all over the city, calling folks to church. The streets were full of happy bustling people. Some going to worship, while others were carrying their Christmas goose to the baker's - to be cooked in his huge ovens; everyone looking forward to their Christmas dinner.

Quickly the Spirit moved on with Scrooge still hanging tight on to his robe. At last they stopped and slipped, quite unseen, into the home of Scrooge's clerk, Bob Cratchit.

Now this poor fellow had to bring up his family on fifteen shillings a week, for that was all that mean old Scrooge would pay him.

But today it was Christmas Day, and Mrs Cratchit had managed to save enough to make a Christmas dinner - a special dinner that all the Cratchits would remember until next Christmas.

As Scrooge and the Spirit gazed at the happy scene, Mrs Cratchit was busy laying the table for dinner helped by her daughters, while a couple of the younger Cratchits danced round the room getting very excited.

Young Peter was in charge of a great pan of potatoes, bubbling away on the fire. Everybody was simply longing for dinner time.

"Here's Father coming home," cried the two little Cratchits, as Bob came home from church with his son, Tiny Tim, on his shoulder.

Young Tiny Tim was very frail. He had to use a little crutch, and could only walk with an iron frame strapped onto his leg. When he was tired he sat by the fire on his own small stool.

In rushed the young Cratchits carrying the goose that had been roasting in the baker's oven. It was dinner time at last!

The dishes were put on the table and grace was said. Everyone took a deep breath as Mrs Cratchit plunged her carving knife into the hot roast goose, stuffed with sage and onion and served with apple sauce and mashed potatoes. It was enough for the whole family.

Great excitement now as Mrs Cratchit left the room.

She returned, quite flushed, with a Christmas pudding. And what a pudding! It was speckled like a cannonball, blazing with brandy and a sprig of holly on top.

At last dinner was finished, and the whole family sat round the fire with roast chestnuts and some punch. Bob raised his glass. "A Merry Christmas to us all, my dears. God bless us!"

"God bless us everyone!" said Tiny Tim, and Bob reached out and held his frail little hand.

"Spirit," said Scrooge, "tell me if Tiny Tim will live!"

"I see an empty chair," replied the Spirit, "and a crutch without an owner. If things do not change, Tiny Tim will die!"

"No, no," said Scrooge. "Kind Spirit, say he will not die!"

Scrooge hung his head as he remembered how little money he paid Bob Cratchit. It was because of him Bob's family were so poor, so shabby and so often cold and hungry.

That night the Spirit of Christmas Present showed Scrooge many things. They visited places that made Scrooge shudder. They flew over bleak dark moors where miners worked underground. They flew over the raging sea and heard sailors singing carols as they steered the ship through a storm.

Worst of all they saw ragged hungry children with no-one to care for them, even at Christmas. It was then Scrooge remembered that he had never tried to help them, although he had been given many chances.

It had seemed such a long night and the Spirit and Scrooge had travelled far. A bell struck twelve and the Spirit vanished.

As Scrooge looked again, he saw a dark figure drifting towards him through the mist.

"Are you the Spirit of the Future?" whispered Scrooge.

The Spirit did not answer, just pointed. He showed Scrooge people talking about a certain old miser who had just died. No-one was sad, no-one went to his funeral, and no-one missed him or loved him.

Then, without a word, the Spirit of the Future took
Scrooge to the home of Bob Cratchit. There he saw the sad
faces of the young Cratchits, the empty stool by the
fireside and the crutch in the corner. Scrooge realised that
Tiny Tim must have died.

"Tell me about my future, Spirit!" begged Scrooge
trembling, but the Spirit didn't reply. Instead he led him to
a churchyard and pointed at a gravestone.

Scrooge crept towards it and written on the stone was
his own name: EBENEZER SCROOGE.

"That can't be me!" cried Scrooge.
"I will change! I promise to keep
Christmas in my heart all the year
round!"

As poor frightened Scrooge tried to
grab the Spirit's arm, the black robe
collapsed and changed into a bedpost.

Yes, the bedpost was his own, the
bed was his own and the room was his
own. Best of all, he was alive with lots
of time in front of him to change his
ways.

Scrooge jumped out of bed laughing and crying in the same breath. He rushed round the room dancing and singing, so happy, he put on all his clothes inside out and back to front.

Running to the window, he opened it and stuck his head out. "What day is it today?" he called to a boy dressed in his best clothes.

"Why, Christmas Day!" replied the lad.

"So, I haven't missed it!" said Scrooge to himself.

Then he told the young boy to run and buy the huge turkey hanging in the poulterer's shop, and he gave the boy half-a-crown for his trouble.

"I'll send it to Bob Cratchit!" chuckled Scrooge. "He'll never guess where it came from. It must be twice as big as Tiny Tim!"

Having paid for the turkey and a man with a cab to take it over to Camden Town, Scrooge felt quite breathless.

No time to waste. Scrooge shaved, then dressed himself up in his best clothes. He went out into the streets calling: "Merry Christmas" to passers by and smiling at everyone he met.

He went to the church and then walked towards his
nephew Fred's house. He passed the door a dozen times
before he plucked up courage to knock.

A girl let him in and Scrooge went straight to the dining
room and poked his head round the door.

"Why bless my soul!" cried his nephew, "who's that?"

"It's your uncle Scrooge. I have come to dinner. Will
you let me in?"

The family gave Scrooge such a warm welcome that he
felt at home in five minutes. He enjoyed a wonderful party
with wonderful games - the old man never felt happier.

Next morning, Scrooge wanted to
be first at the office (just to catch Bob
Cratchit coming in late).

The clock struck nine, no Bob.
Scrooge sat with his door wide open.
At last at eighteen and a half minutes
past nine, Bob arrived.

His hat and scarf were off before he
opened the door. He jumped up on his
stool and began writing away as fast as
he could.

"What do you mean by coming here
at this time of day?" growled Scrooge,
pretending to be angry.

"It's only once a year!" pleaded poor Bob. "I promise it won't happen again!"

"I'm not going to stand this kind of thing any longer!" Scrooge went on, digging Bob Cratchit in the ribs. "And therefore I am about to raise your salary!"

Bob jumped back.

"A Merry Christmas, Bob," said Scrooge slapping him on the back. "A Merrier Christmas than I've given for many a year. Build up the fire; we'll sit together and talk about your wages and how I can help your family!"

Scrooge was better than his word. He did much more than he promised; and to Tiny Tim, who did not die, he was a second father.

Some people laughed at such a change in Scrooge - but he didn't care a bit.

He had no more visits from ghosts or spirits. And it was always said of him that he knew how to keep Christmas as well as any man alive.

May that be said of all of us. As Tiny Tim said: "God Bless Us, Everyone!"

The ghosts who appeared to Ebenezer Scrooge
that Christmas Eve showed him what a mean and
horrid old man he was.

By being kind and helping others, he became the happy
man that he had been when he was younger.

But did the ghosts really come to him, or was it all
just a dream?

Ebenezer
Scrooge

Tiny Tim
Cratchit

Bob Cratchit

The Ghost of
Jacob Marley

The Spirit of
Christmas Past

The Spirit of
Christmas Present

The Spirit of
Christmas
To Come

Adapted from the original by Anne McKie,
illustrated by Ken McKie.

Published by
Grandreams Limited.
Jadwin House, 205/211 Kentish Town Road, London, NW5 2JU.

Film origination by Columbia Offset (UK) Limited.

Printed in Belgium.

ISBN 0 86227 827 9

XM1-4